This
PJ BOOK
belongs to

_____

_____

JEWISH BEDTIME STORIES and SONGS

The Heart-Shaped Leaf

A Magical Tale for
Tu B'Shevat

Green
Bean
Books

First published in the UK in 2018 by Green Bean Books
c/o Pen & Sword Books Ltd
47 Church Street, Barnsley, S. Yorkshire, S70 2AS
www.greenbeanbooks.com

Hardback ISBN 978-1-78438-262-9
Paperback ISBN 978-1-78438-418-0

Designed by Shona Andrew
Edited by Kate Baker and Claire Berliner

Printed in China by 1010 Printing International Ltd

011926.6K1/B1333/A5

The Heart-Shaped Leaf

Shira Geffen &
David Polonsky

Green
Bean
Books

It was a windy autumn afternoon, and Alona
was making her way home from school.

The park was almost empty, but everything
moved and swayed as if it were full of people.
Even the broken swing that no one ever played on
was being swung to and fro by the breeze.

"Good wind," Alona thought to herself.
"How kind of you to keep the
swing company."

Alona began to feel cold. She put her hands into her
pockets and discovered a big red apple that her mummy
had put there that morning. "Clever Mummy,"
thought Alona.

She sat down at the foot of a
tree to eat the apple.

Each time she took a bite, a leaf fell
from the branch above.

Bite,

    leaf,

        bite,

    leaf,

bite, bite . . .

Alona was worried that if she carried on eating, the tree would be
left completely bare. But the apple was delicious . . .

"I'll take just one more bite,"
    she said to the tree, "no more."

As Alona sank her little teeth into the apple, a leaf fell from a high branch and fluttered towards her.

This one wasn't like the other leaves. It was bigger and golden and it floated down slowly, as if it didn't really mean to reach the ground. And it didn't. It landed on Alona's head, but she didn't even feel it.

She got up and hurried home.

The wind grew stronger, and everything on the ground rose up and swirled around. Everything, that is, except for the golden leaf stuck in Alona's hair.

"I hope it doesn't start raining," she thought. "I don't have an umbrella."

And as soon as she'd had the thought, the first drops began to fall.

The rain came down harder, and Alona ran faster. Suddenly, she realised that she wasn't getting wet like all the other people on the street. She was completely dry . . .

Alona stopped, then smiled. "Thank you rain," she said, "for thinking of a little girl who's forgotten her umbrella."

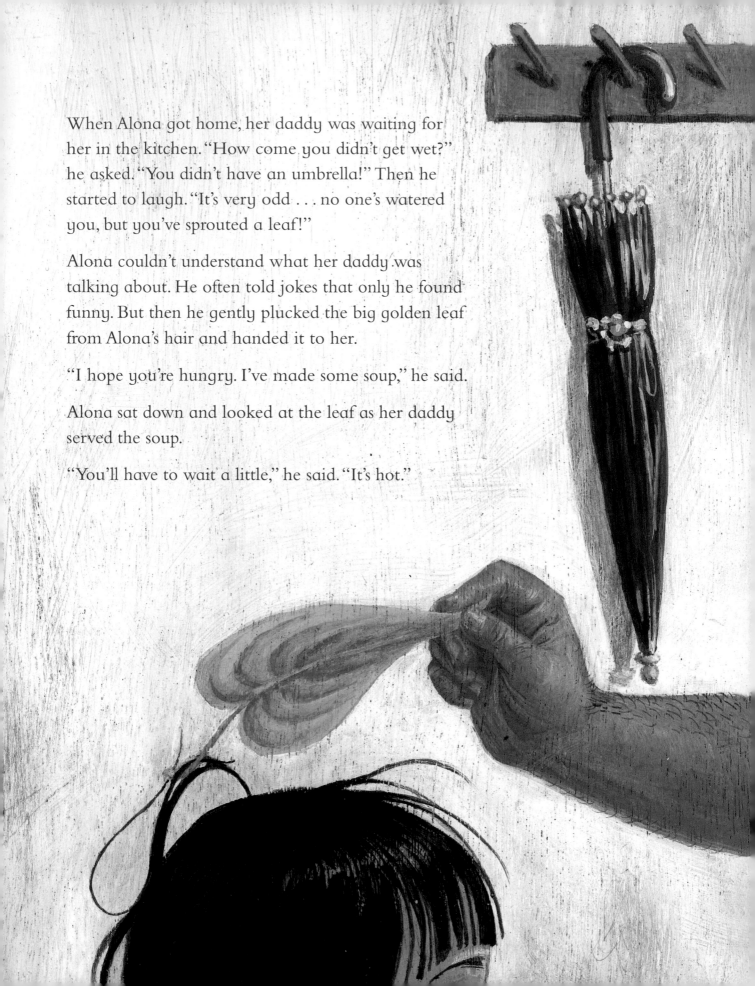

When Alona got home, her daddy was waiting for her in the kitchen. "How come you didn't get wet?" he asked. "You didn't have an umbrella!" Then he started to laugh. "It's very odd . . . no one's watered you, but you've sprouted a leaf!"

Alona couldn't understand what her daddy was talking about. He often told jokes that only he found funny. But then he gently plucked the big golden leaf from Alona's hair and handed it to her.

"I hope you're hungry. I've made some soup," he said.

Alona sat down and looked at the leaf as her daddy served the soup.

"You'll have to wait a little," he said. "It's hot."

While Alona waited, she noticed that the leaf was
heart-shaped. "What a beautiful leaf!" she gasped.
And she wondered who she might share it with, or
if she should keep it all to herself . . .

She brought a spoonful of soup to her lips. It was even hotter
than before. She called out to her daddy, but he was already
taking his afternoon nap.

An hour went by; then two; then three. The sun went down,
and yet the soup was still boiling hot. By now, Alona was really
hungry and her tummy was rumbling.

"Soup that won't cool down isn't *real* soup," she thought,
and she carried it carefully to the sink to
throw it away. But as Alona peered
into the bowl, she saw the
image of a tree.

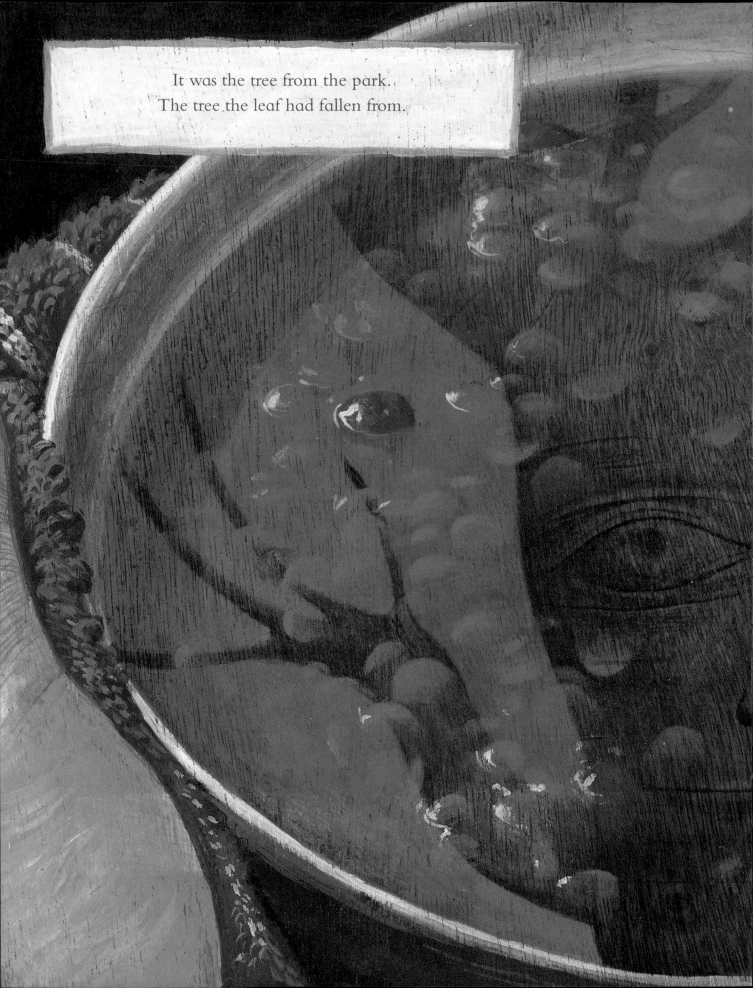

It was the tree from the park.
The tree the leaf had fallen from.

"If you want to eat your soup," said the tree,
"you must give me back my leaf."

"The heart-shaped leaf?" asked Alona, hoping the tree would say no.

"No," the tree replied, and Alona relaxed. But then it added: "The leaf-shaped heart."

"This?" asked Alona, as she held the leaf above the soup.

"Yes," said the tree. "That's my heart. Like all trees, everything of mine is leaf-shaped . . .

I laugh leaves,

I cry leaves,

I dance leaves,

I dream leaves,

I speak . . ."

"Ok, ok, I understand!" Alona interrupted.

"Well then, will you give me back my heart?" asked the tree.

"Of course," Alona replied, "but maybe tomorrow."

"Tomorrow!" said the tree. "Could *you* live that long without a heart?"

"I don't know, I've never tried," replied Alona. "Anyway, how can I go to the park at night? All the trees look the same in the dark . . ."

"You don't even have to leave the house," explained the tree. "Just place my heart on the palm of your hand, stand at the kitchen window, then blow. A heart can always find its way home."

Alona did as the tree had asked. She stood at the
window with the leaf in her hand and gave a long puufffff.
The leaf flew up into the air and disappeared.

Alona turned around and found her daddy standing behind her.

"Is the soup still too hot?" he asked.

"Yes," said Alona.

"Then you need to blow on it."

Alona sat down and looked into the bowl.
The tree looked back at her. "Thank you," it whispered.

"You're welcome," replied Alona,
and added a nice long puufffff.

She raised a big spoonful to her lips.
"Mmmm . . . tasty soup."

Shira Geffen comes from Tel Aviv and is an award-winning playwright, director, actor and children's author. She has written six books for children. *The Heart-Shaped Leaf* has also been translated into Swedish and Arabic.

David Polonsky has illustrated several picture books and also works as a teacher of animation and illustration. He was head illustrator for the animated film *Waltz with Bashir* and is the illustrator of the new, highly acclaimed Anne Frank graphic novel.